THE WAR WITHIN

Mindscapes

BY
Dr. Vanitha Vaidialingam

In the loving memory of

those who have passed into the void

Table of Contents

Perspectives shape worldviews and reflect personality. It builds upon life experiences, influencer impressions, and value systems till it becomes the reality of a person's existence. So, perspectives like habits die hard.

Perspectives fascinate me. It is the driving force behind the actions and reactions of individuals. It is the root cause of personality clashes or even internal conflicts. It is the generator of the war within oneself! If you watch life dispassionately, you will realize that mindscapes resound with bloodless wars in which perspectives are reaffirmed or destroyed!

In this collection of short stories, I have placed my characters in situations where a perspective clash is inevitable. Mental battles wind up to a crescendo and then wind down to affirmation or acceptance. The mindscapes of these characters at a given moment in time enable us to look at reality from different perspectives and cull out powerful insights.

Madan, in the story "Pedestals" strongly believes that honesty is sacrosanct. But he is surrounded by people who are dishonest and even proud of their dishonesty.

Should he change his perspective or will he get an affirmation?

Sanjeev in "The Triumph" has been brought up by a strong-willed, dominating Mother, to believe that rats are vile, dirty, pestilent creatures who must be destroyed forthwith with no compassion. He is suddenly made conscious of the grace and beauty of the creature he is ready to condemn! What should he do?

The miners in "Buried Alive" have little or no hope of rescue. Some hope and some despair. What does the future hold for them?

"Shackles" explores perspectives that are created and reinforced by tradition and upbringing. Should Nirmala succumb to the weight of tradition or grab happiness when she can?

The "Squeeze Machine" dwells on perspectives that are built upon assumptions. How do these assumptions play out?

"The Precipice" is all about trying to put oneself in another's shoes and reliving the last moments of a desperate man.

Fear of a dominant perspective steeped in tradition is the burden of "The Birth". Will the personality clash and destroy all happiness?

"The Seeding" explores the impact of childhood events on human relationships and the "Yogi" leaves the reader gasping as the Journalist is left floundering to firm up his perspective on what just happened!

In a sense, this collection of short stories celebrates life as it is. The stories attempt to define an insight and understand the factors that make the character tick. The characters are fixated upon certain ideas and attempt to analyze situations from a specific perspective. They map and identify the conflicts or encapsulate the personal/social dilemma based on what they consider the norm. The conflicts they encounter force them to recognize/ unrecognize the relevant causes of their significant worldview and evaluate/destroy the impact of the same. They challenge or are challenged to defy existing assumptions, perceptions, and conventions so that they obtain insights with viable differentiation points. All of them end up celebrating life in their unique way.

If you have read this preface, you have taken the first step towards making an "emotional investment" in this collection. Do read on and let me know how you feel about the journey and the characters you encounter. Did they affirm or alter your perspective?

Do comment on the book on the various e-book sites that have published the work. It will help new readers embark or desist from pursuing the journey, that left you feeling the way it did! Thank you.

Madan always prided himself on his honesty. He wore it like a badge for everyone to see and applaud. So, he was surprised to overhear this particular conversation between two passengers, that morning, on the bus.
"The bastard is honest! He is also rules-minded! He will never understand our need and take the practical course."
"I see. What shall we do? Is it possible to pressure him from the top?"

Madan turned around to look at the conversationalists as the first speaker replied: "He takes pride in being honest. He may not succumb. We could try!"

"God! What is the world coming to?" wondered Madan. "Is honesty so bad a thing? Something to be relegated to…impractical?" He could not digest it. He longed to confront the two men and demand of them an explanation. But shock held him immobile, mute…dumbly staring as the two men disembarked at the next bus station and walked away still arguing about the impossibility of being practical around honest men…

Madan was restless throughout the day. He could not complete the tasks assigned to him. Every file he picked up seemed to scream at him "You are a difficult person to deal with. Why are you applying the rules so rigidly? Why are you so impractical?" He wondered what people said of him behind his back. "Did his subordinates resent his honesty? Did his seniors consider him a hurdle in their functioning?" He glanced around his office uncertainly. He had a seat in the center of a busy hall. There were fifty people around him, all busily engaged in completing the assigned tasks of the day or just wasting time reveling in doing nothing.

There, at the corner near the window sat Sharma, who was notorious for the amount of money he raked in by way of bribes. Clients seemed to love Sharma. Most people, who entered the hall for some work or the other, did not like to leave the place without having a word with Sharma. He greeted them with the arrogance of a monarch and waved away their humble thanks for services done with winks, nods, and smiles. Madan hated to watch the cringing, obsequious clients slipping their baksheesh into his hands while he winked, nodded, and dismissed them with kingly arrogance. "What did they see in the man?" He wondered for the umpteenth time. His pan-stained lips and white khadi kurta (fine handloom cotton that is hand woven), straining to contain his protruding stomach was repulsive.

To the left of Sharma, was Mrs. D'Souza who spent the day, loudly denouncing Sharma and his dealings while she quietly pocketed the sums that were handed over to her-- inserted into the files by slyly ambitious clients. Her fat, flabby body was always encased in the floral frocks that barely covered her elephantine thighs and was a garish splash on the otherwise sober scene of the drab, grey office. Her round face with its bull-dog hanging flesh vibrated with the power of the sounds that emanated from her mouth as she declaimed the dishonesty of others and the wonderful honesty, she thought should be the norm in the world. She was a hypocrite and proud of it. She had no illusions about right and wrong. She was a good Christian willing to serve the needs of others to the best of her ability and for the value, they attached to the service.

Next to her was Nitin. Nitin was too lazy to work or even make any extras for himself or his family. He was content to let work pile up on his desk till his manager reassigned the task to another clerk in the section in frustration. He just lounged there drinking endless cups of tea, holding forth on the evils of corruption and how the corrupt would one day come by their deserts. Most workers on the floor had learned to ignore Nitin. They were not even willing to waste their energy being contemptuous of him. They just let him lie there talking to everyone on the floor and no one in particular. He was neither honest nor dishonest. He was immoral. Madan did not like to think about him.

Then, there was that man—Santhanam--who was the President of the Workers Union. How that man loved to boss around and collect blood money from union members who wanted a transfer or did not want a transfer or wanted to be posted to a "lucrative seat". He told everyone with a sympathetic smile plastered on his face "I am honest with you. Not a single paisa you give me will go into my pocket! But what can I do? The bosses demand money to grant the favors you ask! I have to pay them if you want your work done!"

Someone had pointed out the palatial building that Santhanam had built in the heart of the city for himself and his family. The person had also told him about the number of banks in which Santhanam had accounts, lockers, and whatnot...But, he was regarded as a practical man and everyone liked to socialize with him for his benefit. None of them were his friends.

Madan, himself had no friends among his co-workers. When they (the co-workers) had official business with him, they tried to ensure that he did not hold the aces for the deal and he would not in any way disrupt their dealings with the clients by his "honesty". He knew that many of the clients paid Sharma and Mrs. D'Souza for getting work done with him (Madan) as they did not want to approach him directly. He was troubled by it often but had thought that so long as they did not ask him to subvert rules and bend policies, he was ok with it.

Now, he wondered what they thought of him and his moralistic attitude to work. "How did these people regard his "honesty"?" He had never attempted to understand them before, so he did not know where to begin the analysis. He had crowned himself in his mind as an honest person and mounted his self-image on a mental pedestal that he had thought, "This, must surely draw admiring glances?" Now, looking around him he was not so sure. The world seems to be judging him by standards, not of his making. He had condemned the world's standards without examining them or even wondering how he would be evaluated based on those standards. He had moralized on those very standards and dismissed them as irrelevant to his existence. But it seemed that the standards had not dismissed him. They had come back with a vengeance and had deigned to sit in judgment on tenets he had considered impregnable and unassailable!

Madan watched Sharma conduct his daily routine across the room. His soul cringed while Sharma demanded money from a client as if it were a matter of right and argued with him on what can be considered the right value for the execution of the task. He thought miserably, "I am sure I cannot ask anyone for money—that too, for doing what was a duty I am paid for by the Government. So, what is the alternative to escaping the stigma of being honest? Bend rules? Bypass procedures to favor someone? I do not think I can bring myself to do that either! So, where does that leave me? Right where I started!"

Suddenly, Jamila, the room attendant to the big boss was standing before him. "Madanji, Narayan Sahib is calling you," She said with great respect. "I think he has good news for you! He was smiling and looked very excited. He had some paper in his hand. Are you due for some promotion?"

Madan smiled and said, "No Jamila. I do not know why he is calling me. Let me find out."

As he walked to Mr. Narayan's room at the other end of the hall, Madan could not help wondering "What does Mr. Narayan think of me? Does my honesty irk him too?" Mr. Narayan's room was beautiful. It was all glass and brass. The cups that had been won by various members of the sports team stood proud in the showcase specially built for them. Mr. Narayan's medals and trophies stood triumphant on the table next to the window. The rows and rows of legal tomes that lined the bookshelves decoratively scattered around the room gave it an air of distinction. The soft red pile of carpet sank the feet almost an inch deep into its fibers. The highly polished table was topped with a glass that shone from Jamila's daily efforts at cleaning it to a sparkle. Mr. Narayan himself was a dapper little man with a balding white head and a pencil mustache. He looked like an accountant and was one of the best that the department had ever had.

"Sir, Jamila said you wanted to see me?" said Madan hesitating at the door.

"Yes, yes Madan. Come in," said Mr. Narayan in an excited accent. "Please take a seat."

Madan was surprised. Mr. Narayan did not ask anyone to sit in his presence unless the person was a client or an important visitor. He sat down tentatively at the edge of the soft red-colored chair indicated.

"Mr. Madan, did you know that you have been selected as a part of a delegation that is going to study the functioning of our counterpart in the US Government? Your name has been highly recommended by many senior officers. They say that you know the work rules like the back of your hand and that you are very meticulous in implementing them correctly and in the spirit in which they have been framed. Our clients also have nothing but praise for you. They say that they can expect to get their work done efficiently and on time if they have to deal with you. So, our board has decided that you will be the best person to assist us in the study of the work being done by our counterparts in the US and to implement the best practices you find there in our organization. How soon can you be ready to start?"

Madan was elated. It was almost as if he had found an answer to the question that had been worrying him all day. Not everyone considered honesty impractical. Honesty and rule-mindedness brought with them their rewards....

He walked back to his seat with new determination straightening his spine and lending dignity to his otherwise stooping, limp figure. A smile lit up his face as he saw Jamila waiting expectantly near his seat. "Madan sahib, did you get a promotion?" She asked with a conspiratorial smile. "No Jamila, Narayan Sahib is sending me to the USA to study the office there." He said.

"Arre Sahib, that is really good news. You deserve it. You are the only honest person in this office. Everyone else here is a rascal. They are not interested in work. They are interested only in trading their skills for money and also getting paid for cheating on the Government!"

Madan smiled in quiet satisfaction...He was not wrong, after all...

The Triumph

Sanjeev stared at the little creature lying prone on his brand-new pastel carpet. A little black blob is like a stain on the lovely patterns! "Is it alive?" he mused bending down to look closely at the creature. He saw its tail twitch in panic feebly and its whiskers move as the rat caught the scent of the human. But it seemed too weak to move... Sanjeev straightened up and glared at the hapless rodent. How he hated rats!

He had been conscious of this visitation for some time now. The Rat had toppled the waste paper baskets and had nibbled through a few tomatoes and potatoes in the kitchen. Sanjeev had mumbled and grumbled as he had thrown away the food. Rats, he had been told, lived in gutters and foraged through dustbins and were harbingers of the plague! How he hated the idea of them plunging their dirty teeth into his food and wandering around in his spotless, dust-free apartment—an apartment he was proud of! An apartment that was admired by everyone and praised even by his cleanliness-fanatic mother!

He remembered with near panic, how the very thought of his mother had galvanized him into action. How would he be able to explain to her the presence of such an unwanted creature in his home? "Oh God," he thought "I have to get rid of the creature before she visits me next! I can't bear to hear her lecture on cleanliness and godliness another time. It is now like a background refrain to my life. Why must this little rat disrupt my life like this?"

Sanjeev recalled how he had obsessed about the process of catching the rat and groaned at the recollection of hours he had spent searching the Internet, consulting with friends. He re-lived the sleepless nights that dragged on while he planned his different moves. He had set traps, left rat poison around the house, and done everything he could think of or had been advised to do. But the creature had been too clever for him. It had nimbly evaded the traps and had avoided nibbling on the rat poison. It merrily tumbled dustbins and even sported in and out of pots and pans in the kitchen driving him frantic with worry. Finally, in desperation, he decided to starve the creature out of the house.

What a lot of time and energy wasted on one little ugly, dirty creature! Looking back, he felt a grim satisfaction that he had achieved what he had set out to do. He had spent hours every day, mopping up every single crumb that had fallen on the table; the floor, or had been dropped on the kitchen platform. He locked away all the fruits and vegetables in airtight cans and blocked every single crevice through which the rat could enter the food stores. Though it was a lot of work, it paid off. The rat had starved and now it lay helplessly thin and hopelessly defeated before him.

Now it was up to him to deal with his enemy. "Shall I just chuck you out of the window?" He asked aloud. The rat did not respond.

Sanjeev crossed to the window and looked out to check where he could fling the creature. A cat sat smugly on the windowsill licking its lips as if waiting for the readymade meal to be chucked into its waiting jaws. A gruesome image of the unconscious rat arching through the air and into the mouth of the waiting cat rose in his mind's eye. Sanjeev recoiled. He could already hear the cat crunching on the rat's bones and extinguishing the life within the feeble body. "Surely, God will not forgive me, if I do that!" his mind screamed.

He quickly shut the window and crossed the room to stare down at the rat again. "What shall I do with you, you dirty creature," He asked. The rat seemed to respond. One paw was raised almost in a pleading gesture and

Sanjeev stepped back in alarm. He turned away to sit on the sofa at the end of the room to think the situation through. "If I fling this poor creature out of the window in its present condition, it will surely die. It will not be able to save itself from cats and other predators. Now that this rat has surrendered to me, I must show pity. Maybe I can feed it and give it sufficient energy to escape predators before I leave it in the neighboring park to fend for itself."

He got up with the resolution and rummaged through his medicine chest for the little plastic filler. He got out a small glass of milk from the fridge and placed the items on his table like a Doctor readying the operating table. He then put on a plastic glove and picked up the rat. The creature kicked and bucked like a maniac creature for a few minutes and then seemed to lose its energy abruptly. The weeks of food deprivation had taken its toll and it seemed resigned to its fate. As Sanjeev held the creature in a gentle but firm grip, he could feel the little heart racing in panic and the warmth of its tiny perfect body through the plastic glove in his hand. He suddenly felt sorry for the poor creature. "It is after all a life. I may not like it but it is still God's creation. I must be gentle" he thought.

He lifted the tiny rat to eye level and stared at its tiny pointed nose and beady black eyes. A strange need to comfort the creature welled up in him. Gently, soothingly, he began talking to the rat: "Ratty don't worry. I am not going to kill you. I am only going to feed you". The soothing tone of voice seemed to create magic. The little creature's racing heart slowed its beat and the eyes looked at him with seeming trust. Sanjeev picked up the filler and dipped it into the milk and sucked in a few drops. He squeezed the rat's mouth open and put a few drops in, all the time looking into the soulful eyes that stared at him unblinkingly.

As the rat sucked at the milk, Sanjeev felt drawn to the little thing nestling so trustfully in his palm. He felt a motherly pleasure well up from somewhere deep within him... "How could I have thought of destroying this creature?" he wondered. Sanjeev instinctively stroked the rat with his ungloved right hand. The soft silky fur felt wonderful under his exploring fingers. The rat half closed its eyes as his fingers moved up and down its back.

Sanjeev marveled at the perfection of its tiny pink-tipped paws and traced the grace of its cone-shaped nose. "God, you are beautiful!" he exclaimed and gently set the rat on the soft whiteness of the sofa he had so painstakingly cleaned just a few hours ago and settled down next to it admiringly. The rat curled up into a tiny ball and fell asleep as Sanjeev sat entranced...

All that is now left to us, is our thoughts. The world that exists above ground continues to exist in our minds- a memory. We are yet to write it off as a distant dream and live in the moment of darkness and slowly ebbing hope. You see, we—the forty of us—were the unfortunate who could not escape when the mine collapsed. We are buried alive.

In the distance, the rumbles and tumbles of rocks and earth seem to continue unabated. Now and then we hear the thump of a rock in the deserted tunnels. Every fall startles us and panics our hearts. What if we were never rescued? What if the rock falls became so dense that no one can get through them for days or even months?

But the thought of not being rescued is intrusive; draining. I know, it does not help us any. We cannot help but be aware that far above us the world is rotating on its giddy axle with—perhaps--no thought for the men who wait patiently in its depths for a rescue party that may never come.

"But would our kinsmen, abandon us?", we wonder and cling to hope. But the thought will not hush. Time and again, someone is compelled to say it aloud. Others hastily and loudly, admonish the person for displaying such poor faith in our fellowmen. But deep-down doubt gnaws at our souls and fills us with despair. We know that the naysayers are only expressing the fear that is trembling on our lips. But we have to suppress the thought and keep our hopes from flagging. It is important for our survival.

I listen to the survivors talking feverishly—thanking God that they had survived the disaster and bemoaning the loss of their friends and fellow workers. I am amazed that a few miners find it comforting to contemplate on future courses of action. They declare vehemently "I will never come down a mine shaft again in my life! I will try to find some other kind of employment above ground!" Others of their ilk nod their heads in agreement and begin to discuss the relative merits of jobs they could hold down.

I watch the most enterprising of the group, go to the entrance of the cave and discuss the merits and demerits of alternate courses of action for our rescue.

I feel a kinship with them. I want to join them. It will keep us from thinking about the hopelessness of the situation. It will give us something to do. But they return to a corner of the cave declaring "We will wait for some more time. If no one comes to our rescue in an hour or so, we will rescue ourselves".

As the minutes build up into hopeless hours and the hours grow into seemingly endless days, conversation peters into silence. Our silence screams our appeal. Talk seems a meaningless exercise when we are faced with slow but sure death. With every passing minute, we are almost certain in our minds that our families have given us up for dead. We are equally certain that our masters are unlikely to spend few thousand in rescuing miners who they knew could not have survived the onslaught of earth and rock... Thoughts of the world above, wring our hearts and make us long to be back above ground-- even if it was for a few seconds. We long to hear the happy laughter of people going about their daily lives and to feel the warmth of the sun on our skin or see again, the colors that are revealed as the sun travels across the sky. We long to enjoy once more, the play of light and shadows as the trees sway in the wind and create patterns on the grass. We conjure up images of buildings that loom over the landscape and cast deep, cool shadows on the ground below them. We are very conscious of all that we have taken for granted; all that we have not paused to appreciate or enjoy in our hurry to be doing this or that… All that we can see now is darkness—darkness that seems never-ending; ever-deepening. The electric supply has been cut off as wires were downed by falling earth. Most of the men had wasted the batteries of the mining gear in the initial hours drawing comfort from the light. I had switched off my headlamp with a vague desire to conserve the battery for some undefined need.

As we waited in the dark, I knew with certainty that the passage of time was an infallible indicator in such situations. The longer we waited the less were the chances of a rescue party arriving. I became more and more certain--with every passing hour--that no one was coming for us. We had to rescue ourselves! We had been given up for dead! I finally, concluded that there is no point in waiting. Appealing to the pantheon of our Gods would also serve no purpose! If someone up there was making the effort to rescue us, it was time we added our bit. If not, we could survive only if we made the effort.

I was galvanized into action. I picked up my mining headgear and switched it on. The light flickered heart-stoppingly and held steady after a few seconds. I saw the faces of the miners looking at the light with some surprise. They were all a dirty, mud-splattered group of men, huddling together for comfort and companionship, in what they imagined was the last moments of their lives. They needed to be activated; enthused about rescuing themselves. "Come on folks! We have waited long enough. Let's get cracking! We need to rescue ourselves. Everyone, locate your tools. Let us mine our way out of this fix!" I said with all the enthusiasm I could summon.

A few men stirred restlessly and felt about for their picks and shovels. Others rose to their feet in bewilderment. I went to the entrance of the cave to check out the depth of the block. A few men followed me shuffling their feet and rubbing their eyes. The rock fall had ceased and there was silence all around. Some of the men organized everyone into four groups of 10 men each. Two groups at the front would dig into the mud and collect the debris in the mining pans for passing on to the men lining the length of the cave. The pans were to be passed on till the mud could be dumped at the back of the cave. When the first group tired, they were to be immediately replaced by the second group, and so on in perpetual rotation.

As we started to dig, we realized that the mud and rock had fallen throughout the length of the passage leading to the next cave or the mine shaft (we hoped it was the mine shaft). We wondered if the mine shaft itself had collapsed! But we could not allow the thought to sprout; grow and consume our minds. We could not also afford to just tunnel through the mud in any haphazard manner. We had to dig it away completely from one side of the entrance, for fear of the tunnel collapsing in on us when we tried to move through it.

It was painfully slow to work. Every single foot of cleared space had to be reinforced with available rocks. We knew we had to do it carefully or we would lose whatever advantage we had gained with our digging. To keep our spirits from flagging, some of us took up a rhythmic chant. Others fell in line with our singing.

But there was no drinking water to slake our burning throats and our tongues cleaved to the roof of our mouths and slurred our singing. Hunger gnawed at our bellies and sapped our energy. Soon, only the brave of spirit continued the chant. Others merely moved their arms and legs like zombies programmed to repeat an action endlessly. Finally, exhaustion drove us all to a pause.

I switched off the light to conserve what little battery we had and most of us curled up to sleep. Several hours later, we woke to the sound of digging. I switched on the light and found that a few frenzied miners, unable to grab a rest, had returned to the task. They were digging feverishly and even carelessly in the dark. Perhaps the depleting oxygen in the cave was disorienting them; giving everyone a headache. I certainly had one.

Suddenly, one of the miners at the head of the tunnel shouted! His spade had just gone through space! There was no mud fall at the end of the tunnel! A buzz of excitement filled the cave as everyone rushed to the entrance to peep through the long tunnel we had dug and reinforced. Their tiredness; listlessness had vanished with the resurgence of hope! Though nothing was visible in the dark, a cool wind was blowing down the tunnel and fanning the hairs on the heads of the miners who had managed to head the group.

We could breathe! The heaviness in our heads abated. Someone yelled to me to bring the light to the tunnel. I ran back to get the lamp from where I had placed it on top of a small niche in the rock face.

As the first man stepped out of the tunnel with the lamp, we waited with bated breath to hear the news. There was a profound silence and then we heard piteous sobbing. We looked at each other in dismay. What had he found--

another rock fall? Is he crying because there is no escape? The next man in the tunnel called out "Arrye, what happened? Why are you crying? Have we reached another cave with a rock fall?" The man in the next chamber answered tearfully: "We are in the mine shaft! I can see the night sky from where I stand. I can also see the search teams with their lights getting ready to come down. I am so happy that I am crying!"

We hugged each other in ecstasy and yelled in joy. A few men even did an impromptu dance, while others rushed through the opening into the open space beyond...

We set out from the foothills cheerfully. There was much laughter, some raillery, and plenty of horseplay to begin with. That was normal. Teenagers everywhere are the same. Bunch them together and you will have a riot. We were no different. We laughed, pranked, teased, and joked to hide our nervousness. We knew the trek would be long and hard and most of us would tire. Some of us would plonk down on the wayside trying to recoup our strength and catch up with the energetic ones in our group. Others may give up the battle and return. But I was sure most of us would reach the destination sometime... stragglers and all.

I walked briskly, singing to myself; tearing my way forward through the curtain of steadily streaming wind. The fresh, cold force blew my voice away, dragged my long black hair backward like a flag flapping in the wind, and even tried to push me back down the slope. I felt invigorated, challenged, and adventurous as I pumped my legs and dragged the weight of my body upwards ignoring its antics and defying its power.

We managed to gain height over the hours slowly; determinedly, till precipices to our right sent us clinging to sheer cliff walls to the left.

That is when I noticed Ashutosh. He was behaving strangely. He was weaving in and out on the path.

I hurried forward to catch up with him. "Ashutosh wait up man!" I cried as loudly as I could. He heard me-- though the wind plucked my voice and hurled it down the slope--and waited in the middle of the path till I caught up with him. "What's up?" I queried with genuine concern as I reached his side. He cast a sidelong glance at me and said a little sulkily "Nothing! What should be wrong?" I did not challenge it. After all, we were grown up—at least, almost grown up—and we knew what we were doing. Maybe he was just pretending---playing a game with himself? I decided it was none of my business and began to talk about soccer.

The hours gained on us and it became colder as we climbed. Our tired limbs protested as we pushed ourselves forward with rhythmic chants and musical diversions. Finally, we reached the point where we needed to rest. We curled our limbs in embryonic postures and kept close together as we rested our backs on the cliff wall. I dozed off…

***

Ashuthosh stood up slowly so as not to disturb me. He stared fascinated at the sheer edge of the cliff. What did his father feel when he stood teetering on the parapet wall of the tallest building in the city? Did he relive the misery that had got him onto the wall? Did he even remember the little children he would be leaving behind? Did he think of the woman he had married, promising to stand by her in happiness and sorrow? Ashutosh was not sure now!

Oh, how many days and nights he had spent thinking about the last moments of his father --sometimes bitterly; sometimes sorrowfully. How he had hated him for taking the easy way out! How he had cursed him for his cowardice! Did he think he could solve all his problems by merely taking the exit?

He had watched his mother washing vessels and clothes in the neighboring households to ensure that her two children did not starve and had a roof over their heads. How she had urged him to forget all that had happened and get on with life, as she had!

She had the typical fatalism of the Indian woman. "That is my fate. I must make the best of what the maker has chosen to give me," she had said to Ashuthosh several times a day. Ashuthosh could not accept it. Why should she be made to suffer like this? What was this fate she was talking about? To him, it seemed that she was being punished for his father's cowardice.

He remembered how she had wept when the news of her husband's suicide was brought to her. He distinctly remembered her wailing "Why did he not trust me to stand by him?" He had often wondered about that. Why? Why had he not trusted his wife and children in his misery? Did he think that by jumping off the building, he would free them from the mess he had made of life? They had not escaped. They had to pay up the debts with everything they had. The house had been sold, mother's jewelry had been sold and finally, his little sister's tricycle and even his toys had been pawned to pay off the debts. A few debtors had waived the debt—not out of charity—but because it would be useless to press the debts and expensive to drag it all through courts. At twelve, Ashuthosh was left to make what he could of life and take on the burden of living with the stigma of a parent's suicide.

He had continued to attend school as the fees had been paid up to the end of the term. His friends whispered around him and gave him pitying looks. His teachers were extra kind to him and did not berate him when he was abstracted in class. He felt very lonely and miserable—like a freak on show. He was very happy to quit the school and enroll in the free Government school at the end of the term.

No one knew his father or what he had done in the new school. Moreover, such episodes were common among that class of people… How hard he had worked to complete school with good grades. How proud his mother had been of him. She hugged him with tears in her eyes and a vow on her lips "Ashutosh you shall go to college even if it means I work in a few more houses!" How disappointed she had been when he had insisted that he would work during the day and take courses with the evening college. "No, No! Your father would not have liked that!" She had exclaimed catapulting him into blazing anger. He had then screamed at her "Father? Do you talk to me of Father? He should not have left us all to fend for ourselves if he had an iota of love for us! He did not care what happened to us! Why should I care what he would have felt? I care more about what you feel! I hate Father!"

That had happened several years ago. He had worked and studied hard and had completed his graduation with honors. He had won a scholarship for post-grad studies and here he was with his fellow students, enjoying treks and holidays.

His mother had died two years ago —ravaged by disease and sorrow. His sister had married their neighbor and now spent her life being beaten by a drunken husband and slogging for a brood of unkempt brats. Ashutosh had not been able to prevent that marriage. Her mother had felt it was all for the best and had agreed to her marriage because the girl had become pregnant with that man's child. Ashuthosh suggestion that she should go in for an abortion and proceed with her studies had met with a storm of invectives. His reasoning did not appeal to his mother or sister. They had insisted that the shame would be unbearable and that they would have to commit suicide. Finally, in quiet anger, Ashutosh had given in.

Looking down at the precipice that fell away from his feet, Ashuthosh was not very sure that his father had thought of anything when he had stood teetering on the edge of the parapet wall. The depths had a fascination of their own. It drained thought and swayed the body into involuntary surrender to its force. The pull seemed irresistible. His body seemed to instinctively cling to the solid ground, while his mind wanted to experience the pleasure of sailing through the air and floating down the length of the cliff...

~~~~

I woke up refreshed from my short but deep sleep wondering where I was. My limbs were cramped and almost numb with inactivity and cold. I looked around for Ashutosh and saw him standing teetering on the edge of the cliff. He seemed mesmerized by the depths. My mind screamed in panic "What was he going to do? Is he planning suicide? I had heard some rumor that his father had committed suicide by jumping off a tall building. Does one inherit suicidal tendencies? God! This fellow did not need to commit suicide! He had everything going for him!"

I got up quietly as I could. I did not want to startle Ashutosh into falling off the cliff. I do not know how I covered the distance without making too much noise. I crept forward for what seemed like an eternity. I finally had my hands firmly around his waist and was dragging him back from the cliff edge.
~~~~

He did not struggle. He came away like a man in a trance. When I let him go in surprise, he continued to stand in the middle of the path staring at me with unseeing eyes. We could hear the voices of our group as they were climbing up and coming around the bend.

Ashutosh was startled out of his daze. He wiped his forehead with his handkerchief and said gruffly "Thanks, pal. I don't know what I was doing!" I patted him on the shoulder inadequately and we began climbing again.

We did not want to answer questions. I was not sure of the answers and I felt Ashutosh did not want to answer. The sound of our feet crunching the gravel was soothing in the silence of the hills.

After an hour I turned to Ashuthosh and asked "Do you want to talk about it?" He gave me a quick sidelong look and turned his head away for a few moments. Then he said "Ram, I don't know what happened to me back there. The cliff edge fascinated me. I perhaps wanted to relive the last moments of my father. I wanted to know exactly what he had felt before he jumped off the tall building to his death. I wanted to know if he had thought of us at all. Now, I think I know. When you are there at the edge of the cliff, you think of nothing. Your body struggles against a powerful mind. The mind wants to be free; it wants to float into extinction; destroy the body and taste freedom. No ties are binding you to the earth. If you have reached the cliff edge for whatever reason, there is no turning back. The force of the precipice is greater than the force of love. My father could not have turned back once he had climbed the wall...”

I was not sure I understood what he was talking about, but it seemed to have cleared out some deep-seated pain within him. He seemed more cheerful and light-hearted…

~~~
~~~

The thick door muted all sounds and hushed the room in which he waited anxious and tense. He must have measured the space at least a dozen times and had finally flung himself down on the hard, uncomfortable plastic molded pieces of furniture called waiting room chairs. His form was ill-fitted to the dimensions of the chair. The sides poked into his backside and squeezed his thighs. He had to keep his legs stretched out to balance himself in the minuscule contraption.

In a sense, he welcomed the discomfort. His wife was in there having their first baby and he could hear her groans and screams every time the door was opened to admit a nurse going in or a doctor coming out. This was a small discomfort and it made him feel he was sharing something with her.

He remembered the day he had gone to Sheila's house for the "bride-seeing" ceremony. "How long ago was that? Just, a little over a year! God, it now seems like a lifetime ago!" he mused. He had felt embarrassed-- like a freak on show. His mother and sister had insisted on his wearing an elegant Sherwani. He had bowed down to their demands and had spent the ride to the Bride's home sweating and swearing at them for forcing him into the dress. He had mopped his face a dozen times with his handkerchief till it was dripping wet. He had repeatedly asked his mother about the woman he was about to meet. He had a hundred unanswered questions and his mother had not bothered to answer any of them. All his mother had said to every question he had asked was "Ram, don't ask all these questions. They are not material. Just say yes to this girl. You will like her. She comes from a family that is known to have sons in every generation. Marry her and my grandson will be playing on my lap in a year".

He had protested vehemently and pointed out that having sons was not everything. He had to live his life with the woman and needed to know more about her. They had hushed him up and escorted him firmly into the parlor where his future in-laws were waiting expectantly. They had greeted them with folded hands and had seated them in Air-conditioned comfort. They had plied them with sweetmeats and pakoras (a fried savory) and had stared at him covertly as he tried hard not to notice or blush scarlet with embarrassment.

He could see Sheila's little sister peeping at him from behind the door and turning to whisper to someone just standing out of his range of vision. "Was that the girl he was brought here to meet and marry?" he had wondered as his mother elicited at great length the genealogy of the family from Sheila's mother and gloated over the number of women in the family who had delivered only male children.

Finally, he heard his mother say "Can we see our future daughter-in-law?" and looked up quickly at the doorway where Sheila's sister stood whispering. "Why not?" said Sheila's mother and went quickly towards the door calling out "Sheila, come, bring the coffee for our guests." The door had opened and he had seen Sheila for the first time.

The room had vanished. His discomfort in his elaborate Sherwani had vanished. Time had stood still for him as he had watched the beautiful, graceful girl almost float out of the recess and walk towards him with a tray of cups in her hand. "Oh God, she is so beautiful!" he had thought. "Do I deserve her? I am such an ordinary fellow. I am swarthy, built on gigantic lines and she is like a gazelle! What if she refuses to marry me?" He had been trembling when she had handed him his cup and had momentarily lifted her eyes to gaze at him. She had then turned away to serve his parents and then seat herself on a settee next to his mother. He had followed her movements and had continued to gaze at her with unblinking eyes, till his sister had nudged him and whispered "Don't behave like a star-struck teenager. Close your mouth and act dignified. You are the groom here!"

He quickly looked away in embarrassment and focused his entire attention on consuming the coffee that she had served him. When he dared to look up and steal a sidelong glance at her, he found her looking at him with a mischievous smile dancing on her lips. He had loved her at the moment and had decided to say yes to the marriage. The rest was history.

The last year had been blissful. They had decided to have a family almost immediately. What had proven to be a source of irritation was his mother's conviction that Sheila would produce the much-wanted grandson at the very first attempt because she came from a family that had a strong male gene.

He had argued with her endlessly about it in vain. He even pointed out that the gender of the child was determined by the strength of the Y chromosome of the father and that the mother had nothing to do with it. But all explanations had fallen on deaf ears. When Sheila had announced her pregnancy, his mother had set about getting together all little-boy clothes and toys.

He had tried to laugh at her and bring her to her senses. But she had refused to accept the fact. Now he was afraid of the outcome of the labor. "What if it is a girl? Will amma be heartbroken?" he wondered. "Will her relationship with Sheila change? Will the favored daughter-in-law lose her status?" He was sure his aunts and uncles would not hesitate to point out the fact that her daughter-in-law had disproved her theory and even laugh at her. A few relatives may even snicker behind her back and anger her into taking out some ire on Sheila. He looked up as the door waiting room door opened and his mother stepped into the room with a flask of tea and some eats for him.

"Any progress?" She asked in a whisper. "No," said Ram still wondering how she would react to a girl child. Both of them turned towards the labor room door as the Lady Doctor came out wiping her hands on a towel and smiling at him. "Congrats, Mr. Ram, You have a beautiful child. Your wife and child have been shifted to Room No. 203. You can meet her."

His mother quickly queried "It is a boy, isn't it?" The Doctor cast a glance at Ram before replying "Why don't you go up and see for yourself?"

His mother quickly gathered her things and tugged at his hand to make him go up to the room.

As they entered the room, Ram encountered an apprehensive gaze of Sheila. He quickly went to her side and sat down next to her holding and rubbing her hand between his two palms in a comforting gesture. His mother rushed to the crib to gaze at the child. She stepped back with a yelp. Ram looked up quickly in surprise. "Sheila, this is my mother come again!" His mother whispered gazing in awe at the child who looked back at her with the grey-green eyes that were the unique feature of his grandmother…

Nirmala pushed aside the curtain and stood gazing out at the scene in the street below. A marriage procession was winding its way to some unknown destination. The blaring loud music and the dancing "Bharathis" (participants of the procession) provided her with wonderful entertainment. Her flat was close to a wedding hall and there were one or two processions every other day during the marriage season. She looked at the groom seated on a white horse under a swaying multi-colored canopy. He was the butt of the jokes of friends surrounding the horse. She could see the groom bending down to hear what his friends were saying and shaking his head in mock displeasure. Everyone seemed happy to be there. Nirmala stood drinking in the sounds and sights till the procession turned the bend and vanished from her sight. She readjusted the curtain and restored the room to its original dimness before she crossed to the writing table where a single lamp lit up the surface and allowed her to continue with her writing. She sat down in the chair and put her elbows on the table to support her face and chin while she thought about the procession she had just seen.

These processions never failed to disturb her equanimity. She wondered why she ever ran to the window every time she heard the music of passing processions. Why could she not leave things alone? After all, the path she had taken in life had been fulfilling and all those events had happened years ago!   Yet she now and then felt an urge to relive the pain and watching wedding processions was one such urge! Was she a masochist? She would like to believe otherwise.

She had been a happy, contented little eight-year-old when her world had been turned upside down. Her mother had called her away from one of the wonderful fantasy games she had loved to play, to tell her that her marriage had been fixed and the groom would be arriving in two days for the ceremony. She had no idea what her mother was talking about and had asked innocently "Something like the function that was done for my classmate Sita? Will I also get new clothes to wear and pretty chains and bangles to wear?" She had been thrilled when her mother said yes. She had danced away to tell all her other friends about the new clothes she would be getting the next day.

The day had dawned bright and sunny and the "Bharat" (wedding procession) had arrived with the groom seated on a white horse under a colorful canopy. He was a fourteen-year-old boy, looking fussed and sulky. Nirmala had not liked his looks one bit. She had whispered to her mother "Amma he looks so mean!" Her mother had hushed her up saying "Silly child you do not know what you are saying. He comes from a very wealthy family. He will grow up and own all the lands that are now his father's. You will be one happy young bride!"

She had stared at her mother trying to make sense of what she was saying and longing to ask her several questions. But her mother pushed her back into the room and asked the other women in the room to dress her up in bridal clothes and the opportunity was lost.

Later decked in the red silk Ghaghara-choli of a bride and weighed down with jewelry Nirmala had become very irritable. She had been forced to sit still beside a sulky groom who would not even look at her or talk to her. He had even slyly pinched her and made tears spurt from her eyes. She had hated him and had vowed never to talk to him. She promised herself that she would tell her mother all about the mean boy when this function was over.

For now, she had to obey her mother and sit near the boy. As the pandit had droned away in some strange language, Nirmala had felt drowsy and gradually she had fallen asleep with her head on the hard floor. No one had bothered to wake her up. Someone had carried her to bed after the ceremony. All she remembered was getting up in the morning, still dressed in her silks.

The house had been strangely silent. "Where is everyone?" She wondered as she wandered from room to room in her knee-length short petticoat.

Someone had taken down the decorations and they were all piled up in the front yard to be carted away by the decorators. The guests who had come to stay for the "marriage" had all disappeared. Nirmala had finally found her mother sitting at the foot of the well in the backyard crying into her sari. She had run to her mother asking "Amma what is it? Why are you crying? What happened? Are you hurt?" Her mother had taken on her lap and had continued to sob into her hair. Nirmala had not known what to do; or how to console her mother. She had sucked her thumb and cuddled up to her to comfort her.

After crying for some time, her mother finally ceased crying and sat her down in front of her. "Nimi, you are a widow" she had said controlling a fresh burst of sobs with some difficulty. Nirmala had not understood. "What is a widow?" She had asked completely bewildered. Her mother had stared at her in consternation and had said "A widow is a person whose husband has died. Your husband has died." She had looked at her mother with a puzzled frown creasing her forehead "But, I never had a husband!" she had exclaimed. Her mother had given her a tremulous smile at that and had explained "You remember anything of the 'marriage' you had yesterday?" Nirmala had become suddenly animated "Yes amma! That bad boy, who was sitting next to me in that function, pinched me and almost made me cry. I did not like him one bit. Do not ask him to come to play with me again. He is very sulky, means, and would not even talk to me!" Her mother had let out a wail of despair and had given her a sharp slap on her arms. "Nimi don't ever say that to anybody. That boy was your husband. It seems he was angry about the marriage and had run into the bushes in defiance of his parents. He was attacked by a rattlesnake and his lifeless body was brought home in the early morning. You have become a widow."

Saying that her mother had drawn her to her chest once more and had begun to wail. Nirmala had wished that her mother would stop this wailing and crying for a boy who was a stranger to them. She quickly squirmed out of her mother's embrace and rushed into the house to get away from her.

After staying in her room quietly, till she was sure her mother was busy in the kitchen, Nirmala crept out of the house still in her short petticoat to find her friends. As she reached the playground where all the children of the village gathered, a sudden hush had fallen over the boisterous group. They stared at her as if they were seeing her for the first time. She had halted and asked them questioningly "What? Why are you all staring at me like that?" One of the older boys had then shouted "Husband killer! Husband killer! Get away from her. She will smite you dead". All the children had then run away as if they had a tiger on their tail.

Nirmala had stood there stunned and upset. She had returned home to find her mother anxiously looking for her. She had run up to her saying "Amma, my friends are calling me 'husband killer" and running away from me! What have I done?" Her mother had sorrowfully picked her up and carried her inside.

Later that day, the barber had come to shave her head and break the pretty bangles she wore on her hands. Then her late father's sister had come to dress her in a white sari. She had then taken Nirmala on her lap and had spoken to her at length. "Nirmala, since your husband has died, you are now a widow. You cannot go out to play like other children. If there are weddings and other functions in the village, you must stay indoors. People do not like to see the face of widows when they are performing sacred pujas or conducting marriages. You must learn to live your life behind doors. That is our custom."

Nirmala had not liked hearing what Aunt had to say. She had suddenly felt dirty, besmirched, and ugly. Her breathing had become labored and a strange pain had gripped her heart and choked her. She had stared at Aunt helplessly with wide tear-filled eyes and had been unable to speak.

Thereafter, her life in that village had been made hell. She was called "manus" (bad omen) wherever she went and no one would talk to her or play with her. The school had refused to keep her in the class, saying that they were under pressure from the village to prevent her attendance. Nirmala was forced to stay at home all day long, helping her mother tend the back garden or wash down the cows when they came home after grazing. She had tried hard to be cheerful, but she had missed playing with her friends or joining joyfully in the festivities of the village. Her mother tried to keep her engaged with some activity or the other, but there had not been much that could be done in the small plot of land or about the house. She had gradually grown silent; answering only when someone talked to her. Life had settled into a depressing pattern that had seemed unbreakable.

But the arrival of the social worker from the town had changed all that. The social worker had heard about Nirmala's wedding and widowhood and had come to visit them. She had urged Nirmala's mother to move out of the village and create a new life for her daughter.

After much persuasion, her mother agreed to move out of the village, and into the nearby town. They had sold the land they had and had abandoned the house. They had just a bundle of clothes and a few thousand rupees when they came to the town. The social worker had found them a hut to live in and had ensured that Nirmala was admitted to the nearby Government School. For the first time since her disastrous wedding, Nirmala had worn colored clothes and had sat in a room full of children.

Nirmala had determined to keep her widowhood a secret from all those who now inhabited her world and her mother had reluctantly agreed. She had not been able to forget the jeering shouts of her friends and the rejection of the village folks. The images had continued to haunt her and she had worked hard to distinguish herself and prove to the world that she was a person worthy of respect.

The social worker, who had befriended her, continued to support her and help her. She had contacted several charitable organizations for funds and scholarships on her behalf. She had made it through to college with these doles. Today, she had a respectable job and held a position of command.

But all these achievements had made no difference to the fact of her widowhood. Though she now understood the implications of being a Widow, she could not come to terms with it. She had often wondered: "Why should I continue to be punished for a sulky, badly behaved boy who had disobeyed his parents and had got himself killed in the jungle? I did not even know that he was my husband! I was too young to even understand what marriage means! Why must society reject me for something I had no control over?"

She had often and often thought of breaking social shackles and defying the unwritten rules of her circle. She had argued endlessly with her mother on the subject only to be stonewalled with bland statements: "It is not acceptable to our society. You must bow down to the rules if you want to be left in peace." How Nirmala had hated her mother and the traditions she advocated at those moments. But then she had not been able to see any way out of her situation then and had ceased arguing her case.

Now, sitting at the desk under the dim light of the lamp, she realized that she had been given a chance to step out of tradition. Shyam joined the bank as Senior Manager, a year ago. He had been attracted to her from the very first meeting and had expressed a desire to marry her. Nirmala had demurred and had then told him that she could not marry him because she was a widow. He had listened to her story and had then said incredulously "Do you mean to say you cannot marry me for this reason? You were only a baby and the boy died even before you had the chance to realize that he was your husband!"

Since then, he had been persuading her to change her mind and marry him. He had insisted that she accompany him to every social function (functions she had been conscientiously avoiding for fear of bringing bad omen to the families or for fear of discovery?) and she had reluctantly stepped out with him, much to her mother's disapproval and constant mumbling. Her mother had been shocked when she had finally admitted to the fact that Shyam had proposed to her. Her mother had exclaimed "Proposing to a widow! What kind of upbringing does he have?" She had defended him and had brought down a storm of invectives upon herself.

She had been hurt that her mother had not understood the needs of her daughter. She could even now hear her mother mumbling to herself in the next room "What will the family say? They will say that I have brought up my daughter badly. I have not taught her to behave like a widow should and so on. God! How will I face them with my daughter behaving like a hoyden?"

Nirmala felt guilty for causing her mother such anguish. But she had seen a way out of her morbid life and longed to grab it with both hands. "Am I in the wrong? Should I have stopped Shyam from declaring himself?

Should I have been more adamant in refusing him?" She mused. She did not think so. Shyam truly loved her and wanted to see her happy. The villagers cared more for the tradition than for her! Suddenly Nirmala was filled with anger against her mother and the society that had shackled her to a dead body and kept her shackled to it all these years. "Why should I knuckle down and obey a tradition, I know is wrong?" she demanded of herself. "It is sheer madness to call me the widow of a boy who never reached manhood or lived to call me his bride. I hardly remember his face and even the ceremony is a dimly recalled childhood memory. It makes no sense to reject Shyam because of a heartless, brainless tradition!"

With sudden resolution, she spoke out loud: "How could I an educated woman allow myself to be so shackled by meaningless tradition? I will never let society dictate terms to me again. I will live my own life on my terms. I will marry Shyam and become a bride once more. I will cease to be the widow of a man who has been dead these twenty years! Why should I, give up my chance at happiness, for a bunch of people who do not care whether I am happy or not? I can persuade Amma over time. "

She jumped up from the chair and crossed the room to call Shyam and accept his proposal...

The Squeeze Machine

Preeti stood hesitating at the door. Dinesh looked up impatiently at his 8-year-old sister. "What is it?" he asked. "Dada I am scared!" said Preeti, her mouth trembling and her eyes swimming in tears. "Why?" asked Dinesh, concern making his tone gentle, affectionate. "Dada, we are going to the airport tomorrow for an excursion," she said tremulously. "So? Why does that scare you?" "Dada, I have seen the planes that fly across the sky. They are so small! I think they must be squeezing people to push them inside planes. I am afraid of being squeezed and fitted into the plane!" said Preeti bursting into tears.

Dinesh almost laughed out loud at his sister's innocence. A devil of mischief entered his soul and prompted him to tease her. "Ah, Preeti. You are right to be scared." He said nodding his head sagely and continuing with a very serious face: "The squeeze machine does hurt a lot! It is one of the worst kinds of pains known to mankind. But then if you want to fly like the birds you must be small like the birds! That is logical. So, they have to squeeze you. But let me assure you that the un-squeeze machine they use to restore you to your normal size when you come out of the plane is not so painful. It is quite enjoyable. They stretch you beautifully and make all your muscles throb. You may even lose some of the puppy fat everyone is teasing you about!"

Preeti looked horrified at having her worst fears confirmed. She asked tremulously: "Dada is that true? Will they squeeze me? Did they squeeze you when you went for the excursion last year?" Dinesh turned away his head to hide his smile and said as casually as he could: "Of course! Some of the boys cried loudly when they squeezed them. A few cursed aloud.   But it is only a few minutes of pain. You will be all right once the squeeze operation is complete." Then schooling his face to look serious, he turned his face towards her and ordered authoritatively: "Now go to bed, you have a long day ahead. Mummy will not like to see you chatting with me here so late in the night!"

Preeti dragged her feet as she turned to go to her room. Suddenly, she turned back and rushed up to Dinesh for comfort. "Dada, I don't want to go on the excursion!" she said from within the folds of his shirt. Suppressing his laughter, He pulled her arms away from his waist and held her at an arm's length, before he said in mock anger: "You are behaving like a baby! You are a big girl now. A little squeeze should not worry you. They will not kill you. They will restore you too. You should go. It is an experience you must have at some time or the other. So why not now?" Preeti looked at her brother with eyes filled with apprehension.

He was longing to indulge his merriment but did not want to prematurely spoil the fun. He turned away quickly and pretended to be engrossed in his books. Preeti stood listlessly for a few minutes and then stuffed her thumb into her mouth, picked up the edge of her nightgown, and shuffled reluctantly to the door…

******

Preeti stood in the line that was forming before the entrance to the bus. The teacher was busy doing a headcount and calling out names of students who were still wandering around. No one seemed to be afraid. Most children seemed excited. Preeti wondered "Do they know what is coming? Or are they not afraid?"

She felt so afraid that her breakfast seemed to be stuck in her throat and the queasiness in her stomach seemed to be intent on pushing her breakfast out of her mouth. She swallowed hard repeatedly…but there seemed to be no saliva in her mouth!

Preeti whispered to her friend Gita, "Gita, Dada says the airplane people squeeze everyone in a squeeze machine before they allow you to board the plane. He says it is a painful process. I wanted to ask Mother, but she was too busy today. Did you ask your mother about the squeeze machine?" "No," said Gita looking frightened. "I did not know they squeezed you before you boarded the plane! Is that true?" Preeti asked indignantly: "How did you think people got into the plane? Have you not seen planes in flight? They are so small and the people are so big. So, they must be squeezing them to fit them into the plane!" Gita began to cry quietly as Preeti held her hand and tried her best not to break into tears. The teacher hurried up to them asking "Now children what is the matter? Why are you crying, Gita?" Gita explained tearfully "Teacher, we are afraid of the squeeze machine!" The teacher looked bewildered. "What squeeze machine? Are you playing some kind of game?" she asked impatiently and moved down the line to pull two stragglers back into the formation and start the boarding.

~~~

The airport was huge. Gita and Preeti stood hand in hand waiting for the uniformed men who seemed to be in
~~~

charge, to guide them to the airfield beyond the gates. Preeti tried her best to look over the heads of her friends to catch a glimpse of the squeeze machine they would have to enter before they went through the gates. There did not seem to be any machine. But there was a curtained box with a policewoman standing outside. "Perhaps that is the squeeze machine? It looks so ordinary! Perhaps some strange rays were directed at you when you were inside?" mused Preeti as her heart accelerated its pitter-pat.

She pointed at the curtained box and asked Gita "Do you think that is the squeeze machine?" Gita looked at the box apprehensively and said "It does not look like a machine. But maybe it is. I can't see any other thing that remotely looks like a machine here."

Preeti and Gita watched with bated breath as the first student in the line entered the box. A few minutes later, the girl was on the other side of the barrier waving to her friends cheerfully. She had not been squeezed! Preeti and Gita sighed in relief as they waited their turn to enter the box. Preeti had a sudden thought "Gita, maybe there is no need to use the machine on us? We are so small that we can fit into the plane without squeezing?" Gita visibly cheered up. "Yah! That must be it. We are so small that we don't have to be squeezed!" Preeti looked around with relief and watched her friends enter the box one by one till it was her turn. When they were all on the other side of the security barrier, Preeti looked around for her teacher. As she watched her teacher pull the students into two neat lines, Preeti wondered when her teacher would be put through the squeeze machine. "Will she be squeezed to our size? That will be fun!" she thought and laughed aloud.

The lines began moving and Preeti and Gita followed their friends. The teacher walked up to the boarding gate and began talking to the guard. Preeti waited with bated breath for her teacher to be taken away for squeezing….

***

Preeti returned home seething in anger. "Dada, Dada" She screamed as she entered the house. Mother said impatiently "Now what Preeti? Why are you shouting? Calm down and tell me about your excursion!" Preeti dodged out of her mother's outstretched arms and rushed to her brother's room. The door was locked. She kicked at the door screaming all the while "Dada you bad boy. Come out! Come out! You told me lies! The planes are really big. There is no squeeze machine. Even my teacher did not have to be squeezed." She could hear her brother laughing inside and renewed her kicks at the door.

Finally, her mother dragged her away from the door admonishing Dinesh and ordering him to come for tea. As Preeti was placed in the high chair and tucked around with a napkin to prevent her from soiling her clothes, Dinesh walked into the dining room with a straight face. He looked at Preeti glowering at him and asked with assumed innocence. "Preeti, how did you like your excursion?" Preeti said in a fierce indignant whisper: "There is no squeeze machine. You told me lies!"

Dinesh pretended to be surprised and said "Oh, oh Preeti. Your teacher did not take you to the right airport then! They must have taken you to the model airport. They have big planes there. Those planes don't fly. So, they don't have squeeze machines. The real airport has squeeze machines. Only small planes can fly!"

Preeti looked puzzled as she said defensively: "No that cannot be true! The teacher said the airplanes they showed us are real; not models. She said the planes flew thousands of people to different parts of the country every day! But they were big. Not small. We all fit in without any squeezing!"

She suddenly turned to her mother who entered the room with the hot food they were going to have for tea. "Amma have you flown in a plane? Are the planes big or small?" she asked, keeping a wary eye on her brother, who seemed to be dissolving into laughter... Mother looked at her affectionately and said "Yes dear, I have flown in a plane. They are big. They look small because they fly so high up in the sky. You saw one at the airport today! They are big, aren't they?"

Preeti glared at her brother who was doubled up with laughter. Mother looked in puzzlement from one to the other as Preeti shot out of her chair with sudden anger and began to pummel her brother with her little fists....

Jatin watched eagle-eyed as the patient arranged himself on the leather surface of the couch. The man tested the springiness of the couch and then pressed down on it with his entire weight before lowering himself gingerly onto it. "This man is under stress and seems to be suspicious by nature", he mused and made his notes on the case sheet:

Name: Satish Chandra Sen

Age: 60

Build: Tall, lanky and loose-limbed

Physical condition: Healthy but appears to be under stress.

Stress indicators: deep crease on the forehead; tension in the way he holds himself; suspicious, unable to relax on the couch; moves restlessly; seems to have problems trusting people or situations.

"Are you ready to begin Mr. Sen?" Jatin enquired as he pulled up his stool next to the couch. The patient winced and involuntarily tried to move away from the psychiatrist. But the narrow couch offered him no leeway and he desisted with visible irritation creasing his forehead.

"Ah, yes. I am ready. Ready as I will ever be, I suppose! What do I need to do?" He asked peering up at the Doctor suspiciously from the couch.

"Mr. Sen, I want you to close your eyes and listen only to my voice. I am not hypnotizing you or anything of that kind. We will just talk. But I think you will be able to focus better if you close your eyes. Are you comfortable with that?"

"I am not sure. I don't like talking with my eyes closed! I cannot watch your expressions!' said Sen abrasively.

"Why would you want to watch my expressions?" the Doctor queried making a note on his pad.

"Why not? How will I know if you are listening or not?"

"Don't worry about that. I will be listening and even taking notes. You can see my notes at the end of the session if you want."

Sen looked surprised and then nodded before he prepared to close his eyes. The psychiatrist watched the play of expressions on the face with interest.

"Mr. Sen, I see from the details you have filled in, on the form I gave you, that you are happily married and your children are well settled and you have grandchildren whom you adore and who adore you. Yet you are here telling me that you are troubled. Tell me what troubles you?"

Mr. Sen swallowed before he began talking.

"My relationship with my mother troubles me. I am convinced that she is not my mother even though everyone around me denies my assertions. I even had a DNA test done to prove that she is not my mother. The test, to the contrary, proved that she is indeed my mother. My father also told me several times that she is my mother and yet I am unable to accept that as a fact. I can't understand myself".

"When did you first think that she is not your mother?"

"I was always convinced of that. I don't remember when I started to think that."

"Why does it matter so much to you? Has she treated you differently?"

"No. That is the crux of the problem. She has always loved me and treated me like her own son. But I have always treated her as if she were my stepmother. I have repeatedly thrown this belief of mine on her face in anger. I found a strange satisfaction in her pain—almost triumphant. Now after the DNA test of last year, I am puzzled as to why I have constantly thought of my mother in such terms. Even the test has failed to shake me out of my belief. I seem to be obsessed with the thought that she is not my mother. Help me understand Doctor!"

"Mr. Sen, how many brothers and sisters do you have?" asked Jatin rapidly writing on his note sheet.

"I have two sisters and one brother. They are all very happily married and settled. But, my relationship with them is also colored by my belief that they are my step sisters and stepbrother. I never tried to get close to them or play with them even as a child. Now all three of them live abroad and my mother lives with me. It distresses her that I will not voluntarily talk to my siblings or acknowledge that she is my mother"

"What about your father?"

"Father passed away two years ago. Now, my mother is dependent on me for everything. My attitude distresses her very much. My wife gets angry about the way I treat my mother. They have become close to each other and I am developing resentment toward my wife because of her affection for my mother. It is my wife, who pressurized me to meet you for treatment."

"Right. I might want to talk to your wife and your mother sometime. Would that bother you?"

"I am not sure. If you do it in my presence, perhaps I will not mind so much."

"Ok. Please bring your wife and mother with you the next time you come. We can all discuss the situation and understand how best I can help you. Meanwhile, tell me about your childhood. What are your earliest memories?"

"My earliest memory…? I think it is about pushing my baby brother out of my mother's lap. He was just a baby of a few months. I was jealous. So, I pushed him off her lap and he was hurt. Mother smacked me for it and I remember shouting 'You are hitting me because you are my stepmother and not my mother! You would not hit me if you were my mother'. I remember her standing there stunned; her hand arrested in the downward smack. I remember her screaming at me for saying that and crying all the time. I remember skipping out of her way and peeping at her from behind the pillar as she anguished and puzzled over my statement. I remember I refused to apologize to her, even when my father ordered me to do so. I insisted that I had spoken the truth and truth needed no apology. Papa tried to console Mother, but she continued to cry for a long time. I told myself I was not bothered".

"Were you not bothered?"

"Thinking back on it, I know I was bothered. I wanted someone to give me proof that she was my mother and that was not forthcoming. In hurting her, I was only expressing my hurt. But I don't know why I had that conviction in the first place!"

"Tell me more about your interactions with your mother".

"There is not much to tell. I became intolerable and there were daily scenes with me screaming abuses at her and accusing her of this or that. I always blew every single event out of proportion as I was convinced that I had been given a smaller share of something or I had not been given something or the other that my siblings had been given. I did not like people telling me that I should be ready to sacrifice for the welfare of my brothers and sisters as I was the eldest...Finally, my father decided to send me to a boarding school. I was then convinced that my mother had put the idea into his head and she would not have separated me from my home if she had been my mother."

"What happened next?"

"Oh, I went to boarding school and returned home in the holidays. I grew aloof and surly and would not talk to my mother at all. With my siblings, I was very distant. The only person I would talk to was my father"

"Then what happened?"

"Well, I grew up, went to college abroad, and took up a job far away from my hometown. I never visited the family if I could help it. I got married to a girl of my choice and only invited my father to the wedding. Later my wife went to visit my parents and became very good friends with my mother. When my sisters and brother left for the US, my mother had to come and stay with me. I was very distressed at the turn of events and was intent on sending her to an old age home. She too was reluctant to come and stay with me. My wife insisted and nagged till I gave in for her sake. It was she who told me to get a DNA test done to prove how wrong I was. Now science tells me she is my mother. But my heart and soul do not recognize the fact"

"Mr. Sen, please bring your wife and mother on Friday when you come. We will discuss the course of treatment then. We will wind up for today?"

He watched Mr. Sen walk across the room and out of the door…

~~~

Jatin waited with some excitement for the Sens to arrive. They came--the daughter-in-law, leading the old woman by the hand and the Son following behind. Mrs.
~~~

Promila Sen was a beautiful woman. She had aged gracefully and her face was serene, proud…The younger Mrs. Sharada Sen had a homely, kindly face that was attractive. Jatin could understand why Chandra Sen had selected her as his partner. She was as different from his mother as chalk from cheese! Jatin prepared to initiate the conversation as the two women and the man took their seats in front of him.

"Mrs. Promila, I hope you will not mind me calling you by name. There are two Mrs. Sens' here and I have to distinguish between the two of you" He said smiling.

"I do not mind Doctor," she said in a musical voice that had grown slightly husky with age.

"Mrs. Promila, your son has discussed his problematic relationship with you. He seems to have a deep-seated, unfounded conviction that you are not his biological mother. Can you describe to me when he first began to think that?"

"It is really strange. I never did understand why he has developed this conviction. He started to talk very late. He was almost four when he uttered his first words. But, even before that, he would go to his father and everyone else ready and would never come to me when I called him. He did not seem to like me touching him or kissing him. He would cry every time I tried to cuddle him or kiss him. I soon gave it up as it seemed to distress him. When he could talk, he refused to call me "Amma" and would not refer to me at all if he could help it. His father and I tried talking to him about it, but he would not respond. His antagonism increased when his brothers and sisters were born. Finally, we had to send him away to maintain peace in the family. Now, I am forced to depend on him and I can see that he is distressed by the idea. My daughter-in-law will not allow me to leave and my son will not acknowledge me as his biological mother. My presence in the house is a constant problem for him and me. Please tell my daughter-in-law that this arrangement will not work!"

"Mrs. Promila," said Jatin "We cannot run away from a situation forever. Mr. Sen has come to me for help because he wants to solve this problem. We need your cooperation and help. I can understand your feelings, but that is of no use to your son. We will have to go to the root of the problem. Since you do not seem to have any idea why this situation has arisen, I think we must move on to the next step in the treatment"

Jatin turned to Mr. and Mrs. Sharada Sen and said "Mrs. Sen you have been married to Mr. Sen for 25 years now. Do you have any inkling as to why he regards his biological mother as his stepmother?"

"No Doctor. He never told me he had a mother or siblings for almost ten years after our marriage. He never invited his father over, even when our children were born. He dismissed the idea of inviting his father over, every time it was made. He said his father was too busy to come. He would not take me visiting either. I accidentally discovered the existence of his mother and siblings when I ran into a common friend from his village. I was very surprised and distressed. He would not tell me even then. I had to force it out of him. Later, I visited his parents. Thereafter, I visited more frequently and learned to love them all. When his father died, he visited the village for the first time since our marriage. He did not want to bring his mother with us. I insisted and finally, he gave in with great reluctance. He wanted to send her to an old age home! I would not hear of it. He would never tell me the reason for this bizarre behavior. Finally, I suggested that he should go through a DNA test to prove the truth of his belief. To my surprise, he agreed. Perhaps he wanted to settle things once and for all.

Anyway, since the DNA test disproved his point, he has become moodier and quick to anger. The situation has gradually worsened. Now, he refuses to sit in the same room with his mother. Help us, Doctor. He is such a kindly, loving man otherwise!"

"Mr. &Mrs. Sen, I may have to hypnotize Mr. Sen and take him back to his infancy. I think some events that occurred at that time could have triggered this belief that Mrs. Promila is not his mother. I want you and Mr. Sen to think about this and tell me if you would like me to do that. The subconscious mind will remember facts that the conscious mind has forgotten. I will have to put him into a hypnotic state and direct him to delve into his subconscious. You can choose to do it today. If you want more time, you can come back with him next week."

Mr. Sen got up from the chair with a nervous jerk and moved to the couch. "I don't know if this will help. But, come let's get over with it if that is the only way."

Jatin looked questioningly at Mrs. Sen as Mr. Sen arranged himself on the couch and closed his eyes. Mrs. Sen shrugged as if to say "If he is agreeable, what have I to say".

Jatin directed the two women to a sofa and moved his stool towards Mr. Sen's couch....

~~~~

The child stood in the recess of the half-open door vigorously sucking his thumb. The toy seller parked his laden cycle directly in front of the child and said "Child, which toy takes your fancy?"

The Child stared at him speechlessly and then looked at the toys on display with avid interest.

The toy seller pointed to a fluffy teddy bear and asked "You like him? See he even growls when you press his feet!" The child held out his hand for the bear. The toy seller laughed and said "Beta, go tell your mother that you want this toy. She will have to pay me for it."

The child stared longingly at the toy and then turned to go into the house. He could hear a woman's voice admonishing the child for opening the door and stepping out without her permission.

Then a woman came to the door waving him away saying "You scoundrel! Why are you tempting my child with all worthless toys? I know your kind. Your toys don't last even for a day and you demand a huge sum for them! Now go away and don't come tempting my baby"

As she turned to go back inside the child appeared once more in the opening staring longingly at the Teddy
~~~~

bear. His mother called from inside "Chandra, come inside. I am not buying you any toys. You have enough."

The child continued to stand at the opening staring at the toy… The toy seller now smarting under the insults piled on him bent down to the little boy. His pockmarked; dark-hued face appeared gruesome. The child seemed to recoil. It angered him some more. He whispered maliciously with a gap-toothed smile: "She is not your real mother you know. Only stepmothers treat their stepchildren like this. If she was your real mother, she would have bought you the teddy bear you love".

The child stared at the toy seller his eyes welling with tears….

~~~~

The room was filled with sobs as Sen's description of his recovered memory faded into silence. Jatin turned to look at the old woman who was weeping so piteously on the sofa in the arms of her daughter-in-law. He turned to look at Mr. Sen who had sat up on the couch and was staring at his mother with confusion writ large on his face… Jatin quietly closed the exit door--leaving the family a few moments of privacy…
~~~~

He was often seen on the banks of the river. He would talk to no one. He would not respond to any gestures of respect directed at him. He simply minded his own business. He just disappeared into the bushes if too many people gathered at the banks of the river to see him. Some enthusiastic villagers had searched hard for his cave but had not been able to find it. So, the legends grew… one villager reported seeing the swami materialize out of thin air on the river bank. Another said he had seen the swami floating down on a current of air from the skies. A third declared, that the Swami had been seen seated on a ferocious tiger…

Nath did not know whether to believe the villagers or not. He was there to investigate a "phenomenon" for his TV. The program was titled "Believe it or Not" and he hoped that at least some of the reported facts would be proven true so that he could build a story around it. However, he had not had any luck so far. Now winding his way through the forest to the banks of the river, he mused "Can this Swami just be a figment of the village imagination? I have been here for a week now and I have not had even a glimpse of him! I am wasting my time. I will wait out today. If he does not appear, I shall leave in the morning"

As he neared the river, he saw a flash of orange and drew in a breath of excitement. Could that be the Swami? Had he finally arrived? He crashed through the bushes to the bank of the river and stopped in consternation. The flamingos had arrived in the shallow lake abutting the river and that was the flash of orange he had glimpsed through the trees. Disappointed he seated himself on a large rock and watched the birds going about their business. As the sun climbed the sky and beat down relentlessly on the rocks around him, Nath began to feel sleepy. He stretched out on the rock conveniently adjacent to a shady tree and readied himself for a long wait. The tinkling river, the buzzing bees, and the gentle breeze riding over the water lulled him into a stupor...

****

The sun was blocked out by a shadow looming over him. A hairy face peered down at him from above. He looked bleary-eyed at the bits of grass and dirt clinging to the beard and knotted hair for some time without moving. As the details of the face came into focus and his mind registered the features, he was fully alert. The Swami had arrived just as he was drifting off to sleep. He sat up quickly to get his act together and interview the man. As he turned to pick up his knapsack and extract his book, the man seated himself under the tree and leaned on the trunk as if waiting for the interview to begin. His orange dhoti was dirty and torn in many places. But that did not seem to bother him. Nath watched him from the corner of his eyes as he fumbled with the pages of his notebook and poised his pen over the sheet.

"You want to know about me? Believe it or not, eh?" asked the Swami with a crooked smile that lit up his eyes and transformed his face.

Nath was startled. He did not remember disclosing the name of the program to anyone in the village. "How do you know the name of the program?" He asked warily.

"Someone must have told me?"

"That is not possible. I have told no one the name."

"Okay. Believe it or not, it just came to me?" guffawed the swami and continued chuckling "Let that be. What do you want to know? Whether I can materialize and dematerialize? Whether I can fly through the air or ride a tiger? How relevant is that to the world?"

"Those are the things that make the stuff of my program" agreed Nath. "It is relevant to my viewers."

"Ah ha! Your world is limited to your viewers?"

"In a sense, that is true. My viewers like to hear about these things and that is why I go about collecting such information. For the present, they represent the world I work for."

"Good. You know that there is a larger world out there. A world different from what you have limited yourself to!"

Nath stared at him puzzled.

The Swami continued "Do you realize that there is a world beyond the beyond too? A world you have never thought about? The laws of physics it is very different from the law of physics of your world?"

Nath asked, "You mean you can materialize and dematerialize and that you don't belong to this world?"

"No. I belong to this world. Just like you. I just know that there is a world beyond the world beyond your viewer world" said the swami with a mischievous smile.

"Then you know their laws of physics?"

"It is not their law of physics and there is no 'they' or 'their'. All the people who know that world and the laws of physics of that world are people like you and me. They belong to this world only."

Nath mulled over the statement and asked in a puzzled voice "I am not sure I understand."

"Nathji, I am saying that people like you and me have become aware of the world beyond the physical world we know and they have become aware of the laws of physics that govern that world. A few have even mastered the principles."

"Oh. So, you are telling me that you follow the other world's laws of physics and materialize/dematerialize at will; or float through the air or subdue the tiger?"

"I have not said that. I have said that some people have done it. That does not mean I have done it."

"The villagers claim to have seen you do all these things."

"The villagers are creating stories for their entertainment. It is only when people like you come hunting that things take a bizarre turn. They simply believe that they have seen what they say they have seen and get pleasure from the thought. Their belief needs no argument or proof. They do not waste time questioning irrelevant things. Your viewers want to believe but do not have the simplicity of the villager and hence cannot believe. They intellectualize debate and argue endlessly wasting their time. How does your program help them? It just adds fuel to the engine called "time-waster". They gain nothing from the viewing or the debates."

"What would you consider 'good use of time'?"

"Those who work hard and contribute to the world are people who are making good use of their time in the world. Those who realize that the world is ephemeral and go out in search of the immortal are making good use of their time. One is a Karma yogi and the other is a Gyana yogi. You should be a Karma yogi. Give your viewers useful things to watch. Believe it or not, what you are doing is quite useless...."

"So you feel I am wasting my time chasing after strange things for the sake of my viewers?"

"Yes. You could contribute more useful to society. The TV is a very powerful medium. You should choose your programs wisely."

Nath pondered the statement for a few minutes in silence and then asked "Swami it is almost Noon. Would you like something to eat?" As he turned to get his knapsack, he lost his balance and rolled off the rock to land on the sharp-edged pebbles of the beach...

***

He slowly and painfully opened his eyes and stared up at the canopy of trees above him, completely disoriented. He sat up noting that the sun was fast approaching the horizon and it was not afternoon anymore. Had he blacked out with the fall?

"Did I sleep and dream it all?" Wondered Nath as he stuffed his unwritten notebook into his knapsack and clipped the pen to his shirt..."

Should I believe it happened or not?" He looked towards the tree where the Swami sat hugging his knees and found the spot empty... In the distance, he could hear someone walking through the undergrowth...

What does one have to say about oneself? I am a Doctorate in English and have qualifications in the field of Business management. I was a Civil Servant and worked with the Indian Government for 23 years and voluntarily gave up the job to pursue my interest in art, writing, and social service. Currently, I am an educator completely and wholly focused on the betterment of children living in the various slums around Chennai, Tamil Nadu, India.

I have written two other books titled *"Better English for Better Business"*(offline printed version) and *"Close Encounters of the Mystical Kind"* and am a regular contributor to spiritual e-magazines like LifePositive. I am close to completing another book—the title is yet in the works!

If anyone would like to contact me, they can mail me at vanithalingam@gmail.com. I will be happy to respond.

9 798822 356509